TREASURE IN THE STREAM

The Story of a Gold Rush Girl

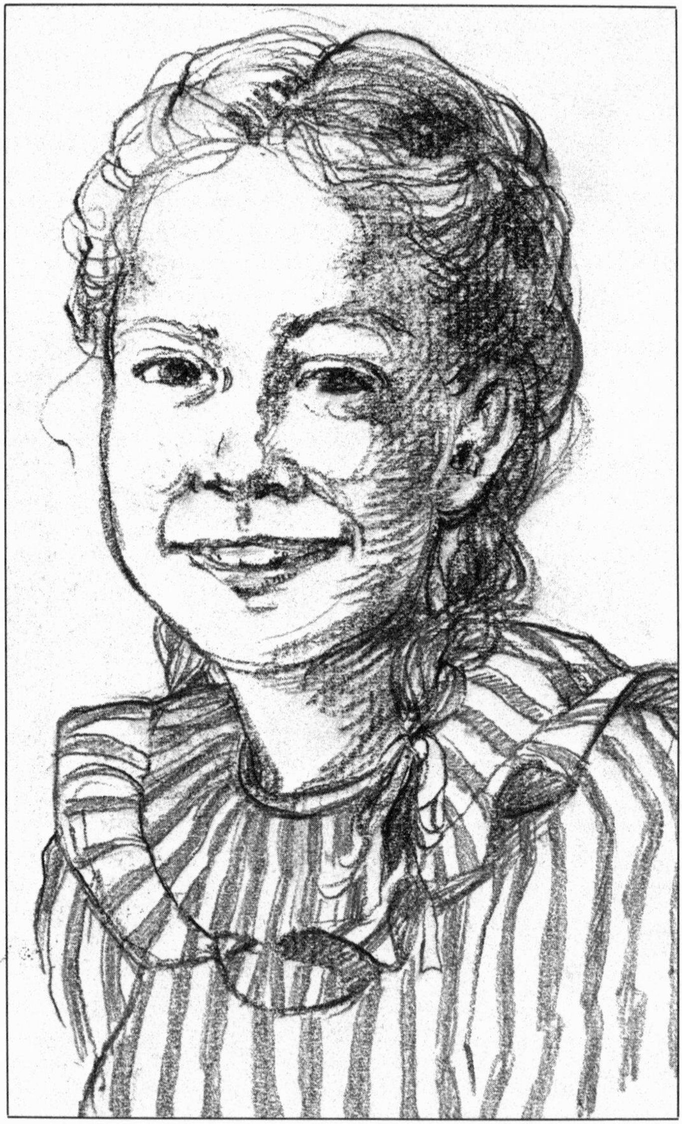

Amy Elizabeth Harris

TREASURE
IN THE STREAM

The Story of a Gold Rush Girl

BY DOROTHY AND THOMAS HOOBLER

AND CAREY-GREENBERG ASSOCIATES

PICTURES BY NANCY CARPENTER

SILVER BURDETT PRESS

**Library of Congress Cataloging-
in-Publication Data**

Hoobler, Dorothy.
Treasure in the stream: the story of a gold rush girl /
by Dorothy and Thomas Hoobler
and Carey-Greenberg Associates.
p.   cm.—(Her story)
Summary: The lives of ten-year-old Amy
and the members of her farming family
are changed forever when gold is
discovered on Mr. Sutter's land.
1. California—Gold discoveries—
Juvenile fiction.   2. California—
History—1846–1850—Juvenile
fiction.   [1. California—Gold discoveries—Fiction.   2. California—
History—1846–1850—Fiction.   3. Gold
mines and mining—Fiction.]
I. Hoobler, Thomas.   II. Carey-Greenberg Associates.
III. Title.   IV. Series.
PZ7.H76227Tr   1991
[Fic]—dc20   90-47180   CIP   AC
ISBN 0-382-24144-4 (lib. bdg.)
ISBN 0-382-24151-7

CONTENTS

CHAPTER ONE

California Dreams

THOUGH THE SUN had not yet risen, Amy got out of bed. She had waited a whole week to begin using her Christmas present. Today was January 1, 1848, the day on which her brand-new diary began.

Amy tiptoed across the room without awakening her older sister, Sharon. She sat at the little table against the wall and opened the diary. She picked up her other two Christmas presents—a bottle of India ink and a feather quill that her father had cut into a pen point. Father had found the feather in the mountains and told Amy that it was from a golden eagle.

She leafed through the pages of the diary. Except for the dates at the top, each page was blank. What would happen to her during this year? She hoped it would be exciting.

She dipped the golden feather into the ink and began to write: "I am Amy Harris. I am ten years old, and I live in California. We came here from the United States, but I was too young to remember the trip. But this year I will remember always, for I have this diary to write down everything."

That was enough for now. She heard her mother moving around in the next room. The Harrises had invited their friends to come for a New Year's celebration. Father said that Mr. Sutter himself might come.

That would be an honor, for Mr. Sutter was one of the richest men in this part of California. He owned the land on which the Harrises had built their small farm. Amy's parents hoped to raise enough wheat and corn to pay him rent.

But the farm wasn't doing well. Amy heard her mother and father talking about it one night before they went to sleep. They had to hire men to help them plant and tend the crops. Almost all their money went to pay them. Father and Mother had hoped to have a big crop to sell, but a storm had ruined most of their wheat.

Father was forced to ask Mr. Sutter to wait longer for his rent. He agreed, but that only meant that they owed him more.

Amy wished there was something she could do to earn money. She and Sharon helped as much as they could. But farming seemed like such a slow way to make money.

She was thinking about this as she walked into the kitchen. Mother smiled. "Why such a long face?" she asked.

Amy shook her head. She didn't want Mother to know that she was worried. "I just started my new diary," she said. "I guess I was wondering what to put in it."

"Well, you can write all about our party," Mother said. "And you can help too."

"What can I do?" Amy asked eagerly.

Mother took down the hatchet from the wall. "Shall we pick out one of the turkeys for dinner?"

Amy cringed. They had raised the turkeys from chicks, and she almost thought of them as pets. Whenever she went into the yard, they followed her around, hoping she would give them corn.

"Do we have to kill one?" Amy asked.

"John Sutter's coming for dinner," Mother reminded her. "We want to treat him well. But don't worry. I'll do it. Why don't you decorate the house with some star strings? I'll call you when it's time to pluck feathers."

Amy was grateful. She enjoyed making the little straw stars that could be strung across the ceiling and over the doorway. It was a Swedish custom that Amy's mother had learned from her own mother, who came from Sweden to America before the Revolution.

Amy took some of the straw that was used to start fires in the hearth. Before long, she had made a small pile of stars. She worked quickly, feeling a delight in the process. Her fingers were nimble, good at small work like this.

Amy strung some of the stars together and draped them across the oak beams under the ceiling. Oak was hard to cut, but their father said it would last a long time, until his children were old.

Amy's sister Sharon appeared, and after a look at Amy's work said, "Hurry up. There's lots to do in the kitchen." Sharon was fourteen, and in the past year she had become bossy to Amy and their other sister Fran, who was five.

Amy took another string of stars and hung it over the doorway to the house. As she stood back to admire her work, her father came through the door. He turned to look and said, "That's good, Amy." But as he went on toward the barn, his shoulders slumped. Amy made a little wish that the new year would bring good times for him. He was such a good man. He deserved success.

She went back to the kitchen and saw the headless turkey hanging by its feet. When the blood drained out of it, Amy began to pluck the feathers. They would save them to use for stuffing pillows and mattresses.

She and her mother and sisters worked hard all morning. Amy and little Fran went to the garden to pull carrots and turnips. Then they washed the dirt off them in the little stream that ran by the house. As they washed the vegetables, the sun reflected off a stone in the bottom of the stream. It looked pretty, and Amy picked it up and put it in her pocket. Maybe it would bring the family luck.

When they returned, they saw that Mother and Sharon had put the turkey on a spit in the kitchen hearth. It was already beginning to smell good.

About noon, their neighbors began to arrive. Sharon's mood brightened when the Kutschers' wagon appeared. Amy knew that Sharon was sweet on the Kutschers' oldest son, Peter. Sure enough, Sharon made it her business to take a plate of food out to offer the Kutschers.

Finally the turkey was ready, and Mother slid it off the spit. "Tell everyone to sit down," she told Amy.

"But Mr. Sutter hasn't come," Amy said.

"He's a busy man," Mother said. "He may not come after all."

He had to come, thought Amy. We've gone to all this trouble for him.

Mother brought out the turkey, its skin crispy and brown. As the dishes were passed down the table, people began to talk about what would happen to California.

When the Harrises had come there, California had been part of Mexico. But two years ago, war had broken out between the United States and Mexico. U.S. soldiers had marched into California. Most of the fighting had been farther south, and the people around Sutter's fort had seen few changes.

"The war is over," Mr. Kutscher declared. "We'll soon be part of the United States."

"That means," said another neighbor, "that California should become a state."

"Not enough people out here for that," a third man said. "And the United States is two thousand miles away. California ought to be independent."

Amy watched her father, who hadn't spoken. She wondered what he thought. Though he read the Bible aloud to his family each night, he seldom offered his own opinions. He said it was better to think than to talk.

Everyone else was talking though, arguing about what would be best for California. Their talk kept them from hearing a horse ride up outside, but Amy heard it. She jumped up and ran to the window.

"It's Mr. Sutter!" she shouted. Everyone fell silent. A stout man wearing a broad-brimmed Panama hat stood in the doorway. Amy had recognized him from his long white moustache. The men at the table stood to shake hands with him, and the women smiled as he greeted them. He knew everyone by sight.

Amy's mother went to the kitchen for another plate, and Amy followed her. "Why did everyone become so quiet when Mr. Sutter arrived?" Amy asked.

"They're not sure what he thinks about California becoming part of the United States,"

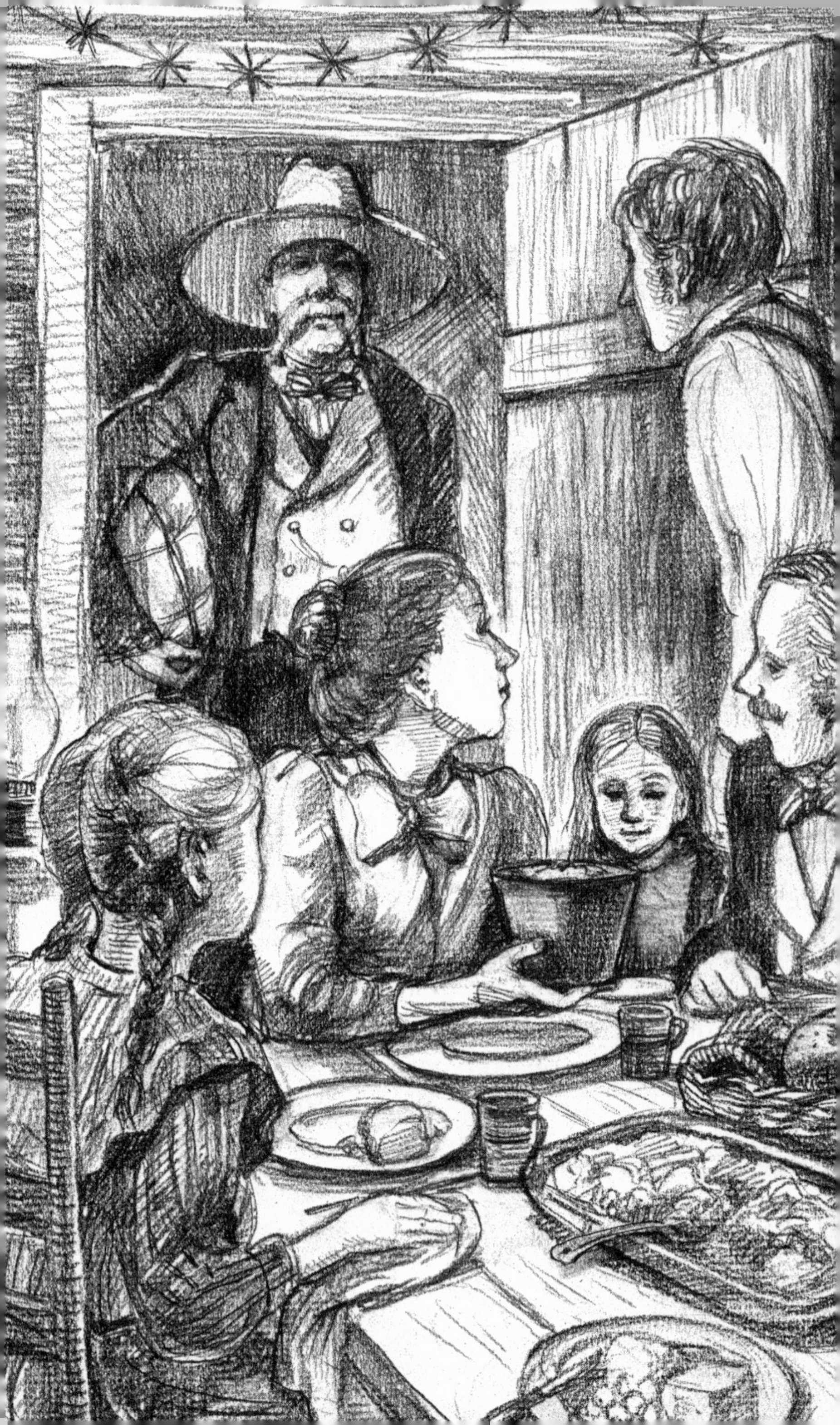

Mother said. "He was given his land by the Mexican governor. People think he may not fare so well now that the United States has taken California."

But when they returned to the big room, Mr. Sutter answered all their questions. He handed a package to Amy's father. "I think you'll want to use this," Mr. Sutter said.

Everyone watched as Mr. Harris opened the package. He held up what it contained—a large flag, the Stars and Stripes. "Time for us all to show loyalty to our new country," Mr. Sutter said.

They all cheered. Someone offered a toast to the United States, and everyone raised their glasses. Amy noticed that there was no more talk of independence for California.

She thought it must be wonderful to be rich. When Mr. Sutter spoke, everyone else listened as if he were the wisest man on earth. Then Mr. Sutter looked up at the ceiling. "Who made these wonderful decorations?" he said.

Amy beamed as Mother pointed to her. Mr. Sutter smiled and winked at her. She felt good. She knew that Mr. Sutter wouldn't kick them off the farm just because they couldn't pay him. He was too nice.

That night she wrote in her diary: "We're going to be Americans now. I'm glad. I know that it will make things better for us. Something great will happen this year! I know it." Much later, when she read the diary, she realized that she hadn't written about the most important thing of all. Something great had already happened, but she didn't know it yet.

CHAPTER TWO

Gold!

IN FEBRUARY, Amy wrote in her diary: "What a day this has been! That stone I found in the stream on New Year's Day—I think it might be gold! But I can't tell anyone I found it, not even Mother and Father."

That day the Harrises had taken their wagon to Mr. Sutter's fort. They needed to buy supplies from the store there. Amy was excited, for there were always interesting things to see at the fort.

For miles around, Indians worked in the fields of wheat. Mr. Sutter had built the fort as protection against the Indians, but he soon made friends with them. He was a generous man, people said, and paid the Indians well to farm his land.

The Harrises also saw herds of cattle, tended by Spanish *vaqueros* on horseback. They wore *sombreros* with wide brims to keep the sun off their faces. Down their legs were brightly colored pantaloons, decorated with silver buttons. As they twirled their *reatas*, or lassos, their blue and red *sarapes*, or cloaks, fluttered behind them. One of the *vaqueros* rode near their wagon, and Amy waved shyly. The man smiled broadly, showing his white teeth below his moustache.

The fort came in sight. It was as big as a village. Only the roofs of the buildings showed above the high wooden walls. At the gate an American flag waved in the breeze.

Inside, people of all descriptions were bustling about. Mule drivers followed teams of animals laden with heavy packs. They carried goods from the seacoast town of San Francisco, where ships docked. A Spanish priest walked by, his long brown habit tied with a thin rope around the waist. He passed two men carrying furs and speaking in a strange language. Amy guessed they were Russian trappers. Three soldiers in the blue uniforms of the American army rode past the Harrises' wagon.

Sharon nudged Amy. "Look at that dress." A

Spanish woman, her black hair held in tortoise-shell combs, was coming out of a shop. Her long green dress was embroidered with thread of many colors. There was white lace around the cuffs and bodice. Amy had never seen so grand a dress. It must have taken hundreds of hours to make.

Many *Californios*, as the Spanish called themselves, had remained after the United States had taken California. And at the fort Amy heard Spanish spoken more than English.

Amy's father hitched up the wagon in front of the general store at the center of the fort. The girls tumbled out of the back, eager to stretch their legs. "Watch out for the girls," Mother said to Sharon. Amy was annoyed. She was ten years old, and was definitely not a baby. She felt perfectly able to watch out for herself.

It really didn't matter, because inside the store Sharon went right over to the fabric counter. Amy knew that Sharon longed for a fine dress of her own. While Sharon leafed through the pattern books, Amy went back to the candy shelf. Fran tagged along with her, and they looked at the glass jars. Inside were striped candy canes, colored balls of hard sugar, licorice, lemon drops, peanut brittle, and broken pieces of chocolate.

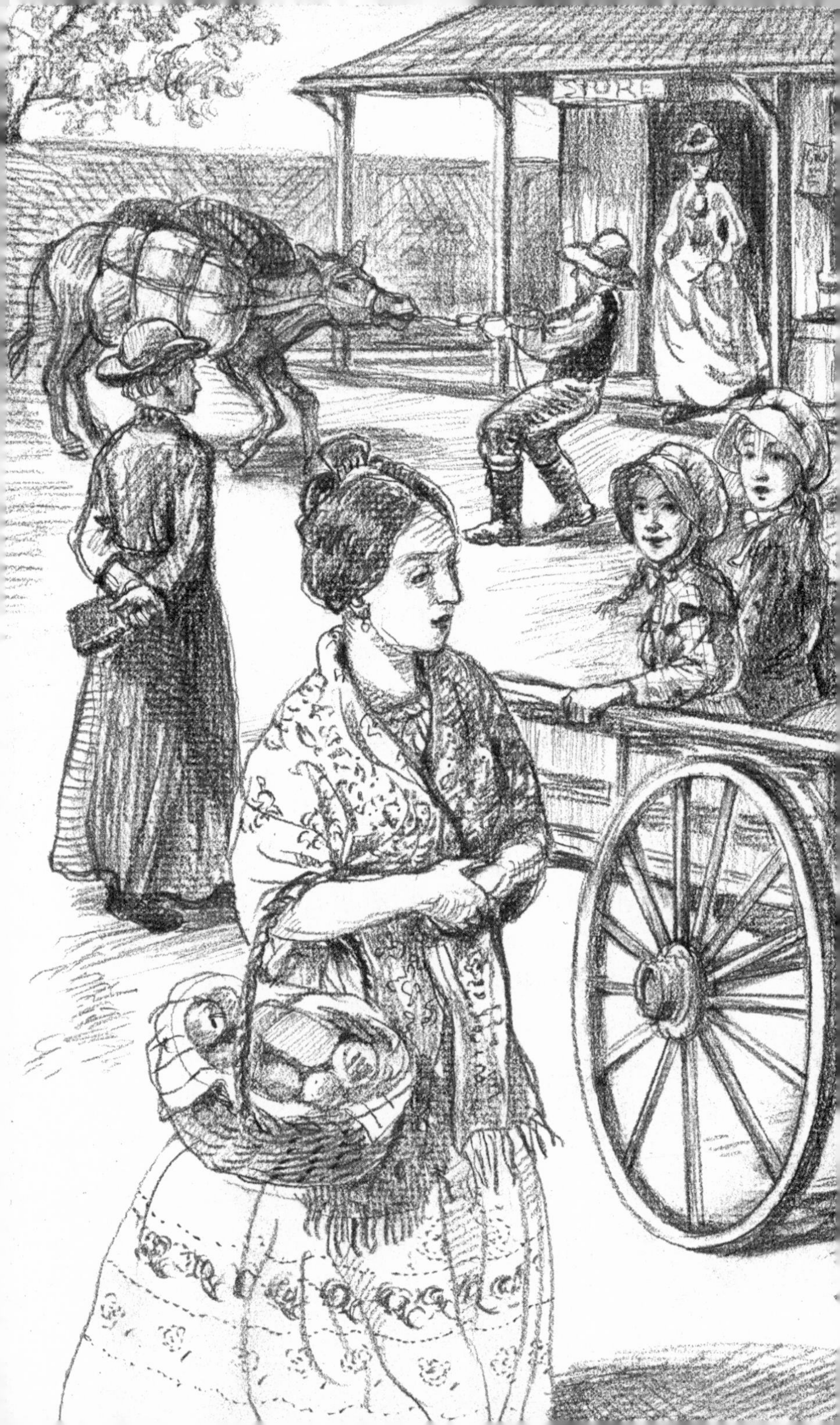
STORE

"I'd like to have one of everything," Fran said. "Wouldn't you?"

Amy hesitated. Her mouth was watering, but she knew that mother and father didn't have much money just now. Almost all their savings had been used up in starting the farm. And they had to buy food not only for themselves, but for the workers who helped plant and tend the crops. "We'd just get sick if we ate it," she told Fran, crossing her fingers.

They wandered through the store, looking at everything on sale. Rows and rows of canned goods, barrels of both sweet and sour pickles, vegetables of so many kinds that Amy didn't know all of them. Then they saw a bushel basket with round, bright orange-colored fruits. The sign over them read ORANGES. Well, that was a good name for them. "I wonder what they taste like," Amy said to Fran.

A Spanish boy was putting cans on the shelves. He smiled at Amy and Fran. "*Muy dulce*," he said in Spanish. Seeing they didn't understand, he added, "Sweet. Like candy."

Amy picked one up. It was heavy, and the skin was tough. She wouldn't want to bite into it.

"Mama," Fran called. "Come look."

"Oh," Mother said. "Oranges. They grow down south, where the weather is warmer. I tasted one once, back home...." She paused. "How much are they?" she asked the boy.

"Ten *centavos*," he said.

"Mexican?" Mother asked, sounding pleased.

He shook his head. "No, no. Cents, I mean. Prices in new money now. We still take *pesos*. One *peso*, or ten cents."

Amy was surprised. That was a lot for one piece of fruit. She started to tug Fran away. But Mother reached into her net bag and took out a cotton handkerchief with a knot in it. She slowly untied it. Inside were a few small coins. She held two silver dimes to the boy.

"Save them for the trip home," she said to the girls. "And don't tell your father what they cost."

Father finished loading the wagon with food and went off to meet Mr. Sutter. The girls wandered around the fort. People were hard at work, making all kinds of things. Amy stopped to watch a group of Indian women working at looms under a little roof. The looms were upright, higher than the women's heads.

Amy was fascinated by how fast the women worked, slipping the threads into the loom, then pulling the bar down to tuck a row into place. The women had sticks with many colors of yarn, and the cloth they were making had beautiful patterns. Amy knew she would have to practice a long time to make anything as good as this.

A group of men stood talking nearby, and as their voices rose Amy began to listen. "Gold, I tell ye. The richest strike anybody's seen."

"It's all rumor and drunken tales," said another.

"Tisn't. I saw a bag of it with my own eyes. Jim Marshall brought it to show Sutter."

"There's been Mexicans telling about gold for years," said a third man. "But you didn't see none of them get rich."

"Well, I'm heading up there today. First ones there will get the most."

"All of it'll be on Sutter's land anyhow."

"He's got too much land, you ask me."

The men suddenly seemed to notice Amy, and lowered their voices. She walked off, pretending that she hadn't been listening. She wondered what gold looked like. She hadn't brought the stone she had found in the stream. It was next to her golden feather at home. The stone had a gold color too.

On the ride home, Mother cut into the oranges and showed Amy and Fran how to peel the skin off. Amy bit into hers. The juice splattered and ran down her chin, but it was wonderful! It tasted like the sun mixed with sugar.

Amy ate it slowly, to make the treat last. Her father was saying something to Mother, and she heard the word *gold* again. She moved up close to the front of the wagon. "Does gold look like this orange?" Amy asked.

Her father jerked his head around. "Why do you ask?" he said.

"I thought I heard some men talking about gold at the fort," Amy said.

All of a sudden, Father pulled the horses to a stop. Everyone was surprised. He turned around and spoke to all of them.

"Men are spreading the story that gold has been found up by the new mill that Mr. Sutter is building on the American River," Father said. "It's far away from here. Sutter told me that if word of that spreads, it will bring hundreds of shiftless people up here. They'll be looking to get rich quick."

Father waved his arm at the land around them. "They'll ruin everything Mr. Sutter has built up here. Gold drives men crazy. No one will work at the things that really matter, farming and ranching. This land is rich without gold. I pray to God that no one *ever* finds any gold."

The girls were shocked into silence. They had

seldom seen their father so angry. He shook the reins, and the wagon jerked forward. Amy sat back and ate the rest of the orange. But she was thinking about the stone she had found.

When they arrived home, mother sent Amy to fetch a bucket of water. She went to the cool stream that bubbled over rocks a few steps from their house. As the sun began to sink below the land, its rays flickered over the wet stones in the stream. All of them looked gold now, Amy thought. But the one she had found was different.

As soon as she could, she went upstairs and looked at the stone. If it was gold, how much would it be worth? Probably not enough to make them rich.

"So I can't tell anybody about the stone," she wrote in her diary. "It would make Father angry. I've hidden it so Sharon won't see it. But tomorrow I'm going to look for more."

CHAPTER THREE

A Flood of Forty-niners

"FATHER was wrong about one thing," Amy wrote. "The news of gold didn't bring hundreds of men looking for it. It brought thousands. Tens of thousands. It seems like everybody in the world wants to come to California."

A whole year had passed, a year in which Amy had many things to write in her diary. In May she wrote: "We saw the first of the gold hunters from San Francisco today. A man from Sutter's mill had run through the city, showing people the gold he found. People left their jobs, their homes, and just headed for the American River. They all think they will get rich right away."

The next month, she wrote: "We all feel sorry for Mr. Sutter. The miners have spread all over his land. There are too many for him to chase off. Besides, nearly all the people who work for him have gone to look for gold too."

The word spread further and further. One day a man with a mule stopped at the Harrises' house. He wanted to know where the gold was. "None around here," Father had told him firmly.

The man showed them a New York City newspaper that said gold was lying on the ground in California, just waiting to be picked up. "When I read that," he said, "I knew the first ones to get here would be the richest. I got on a ship that same day." He had traveled all the way around the southern tip of South America.

"Did you see his hands?" Father asked Amy when the man had left. "Soft and clean. He's never done a hard day's work in his life. He won't last long. Most of these goldbugs will soon go away."

But they didn't. During 1849 they flooded into California from all over the world. People from the big cities of the United States, and then from Europe, and even from as far away as China.

"They're like locusts," Amy's father said. Wherever one person made a strike, soon there were hundreds. Little mining camps sprang up overnight, like mushrooms.

Secretly, Amy kept looking for more gold in the stream. But she found nothing more after the first nugget. "Maybe that's good," she wrote. "I found out that Father was right about gold bringing trouble. When some miners found it on the Kutschers' farm, a hundred miners arrived the next day. And each day brought more and more . The Kutschers were driven off their land."

The Kutschers had stopped by the Harrises' farm to say good-bye. "We're going south," said Mr. Kutscher. "Away from this cursed gold. Someplace where people can make an honest living." Sharon had cried when Peter left.

And gold didn't bring riches to those who looked for it. A lot of the miners "went bust," as the saying was. They saw the man from New York another time, three months later. His clothes were in tatters, and he looked like he hadn't eaten for days. Father took pity on him and offered him some food. "I need a stake," the man said.

"We have no cattle," said Father.

"No, no. I mean a grubstake. Some money so I can buy more supplies." The man's eyes grew crafty. "I heard about a new strike up north, along the Sacramento River. I'll pay you back double next month, sure thing."

Father shook his head. "Go home," he said. "Go back to New York."

The man looked sad. "No money for a ticket," he said. He wandered off.

The Harrises had no money either. Their farm was doing poorly. All their workers had left to look for gold. But the hungry man gave Mother an idea.

"We have a new way to make money," Amy wrote in her diary in the spring of 1849. "Mother and Sharon and I bake bread and pies and take them to sell to miners. Father wasn't very happy about the idea. He says that the camps are full of lawless men. But when he saw how much money we made the first day, he had to give in."

They began to visit the camps nearby once or twice a week. One bright summer day they hitched the horses to the wagon and set out with their wares. At the last minute, Amy slipped her gold nugget into her pocket. She wanted to find out if it was really gold.

The camp nearest their farm was just a collection of tents, some of them made out of old shirts and quilts. People were too busy looking for gold to build anything better to sleep in. As soon as there was enough light to see by, everyone in camp was hard at work.

Each miner had a claim marked out with

stakes and string. Along the riverbank people had marked off sections where only they could work. Last week Amy had seen a fistfight break out. One man said that another had moved his stakes during the night.

Amy took a tray of apple tarts and walked around the camp. Other people were selling food too. She saw a man sitting next to a bushel of oranges. The price was a dollar apiece.

Since the miners had arrived, the cost of everything had skyrocketed. Miners paid whatever people asked, for food, clothing, and tools. They often paid in gold dust. An ounce of gold—just a pinch of it—was worth sixteen dollars. People used gold and silver coins too. But Amy hardly ever saw any small coins, like the dimes her mother had saved in her handkerchief. A dime wouldn't buy anything now. The smallest coin anybody bothered with was a quarter, which the miners called "two bits."

A miner waved at Amy. He was Chinese and wore his hair in a long pigtail behind his head. Amy was used to seeing Chinese people by now. Boatloads of them had traveled across the Pacific to try their luck in California.

This man didn't look as if he had been successful. His flannel shirt and heavy cotton pants were patched in places. He squatted barefoot in the stream, though most of the other miners wore boots. His face looked thin.

"How much?" he said, pointing to Amy's tarts.

"Two dollars," she replied. That was not really very high. Flour alone was more than a dollar a pound. They had made the tarts from their own wheat flour and from apples on their farm.

The miner looked at the tray hungrily. "Too much," he said.

"Haven't you found any gold?" Amy asked.

He nodded vigorously. "Found some, yes, little bit. Need to find more, get rich."

Amy looked at the stream where the man was panning. It looked just like the place where she found the nugget of gold. "Show me how you find gold, and I'll give you a tart," she said.

The man smiled and nodded. He bent over and swished some dirt from the bottom of the stream into his pan. He swirled the pan around, mixing dirt and water together. Then he tilted the pan, washing some of the dirt over the side.

"Gold dust heavy, see?" he said. "Goes to bottom of pan. Then wash the rest away." Carefully, he washed more and more of the dirt out of the pan. Finally there was nothing in the bottom but a few grains of black sand. He tilted the pan toward the sun, studying it. Amy bent over to see better.

"There," he pointed. She saw it too—a little fleck of shining gold. The man pressed his finger onto it, picking it up. He showed her how it stuck to his fingertip. Then he took a small cloth bag from his pocket and carefully dropped the fleck into it.

She gave him the tart and watched as he took a bite of it. He smiled. "You hunt for gold too, eh? Maybe you lucky."

She hesitated. He seemed like a nice man. She took her nugget out of her pocket. "Is this gold?" she said.

His eyes widened, and right away she knew she had made a mistake. "Where you find that?" he said.

"Um . . . far away," she said. "In the mountains." She felt guilty at the lie. But she remembered how the Kutschers had lost their farm.

"Let me see," he said. She shook her head nervously and pulled back her hand.

The Chinese miner shrugged. "Maybe not gold," he said. "That man, he tell for sure." He pointed to a rough-looking man who sat under a tree nearby. He wore a pistol in a holster and had a rifle lying next to him. He was the only man in the camp who wasn't working.

"He buy gold from miners," the Chinese man said. "He know gold."

"That's all right," Amy said. "I must sell my tarts." She hurried away.

She went farther up the stream. The tarts sold quickly. Some of the men had bought them from her before and knew they were good. They paid her in silver dollars, and the coins sagged in the pockets of her dress. When she sold the last one, she hurried back to their wagon.

But Mother and Sharon were not there. They were selling molasses bread and meat pies to other miners. Amy sat in the back of the wagon, hoping they would finish soon.

The rough-looking man suddenly appeared. "Are you the girl who found a nugget?" he said.

She was too afraid to say anything. She stared at the pistol that hung at his side. He noticed.

"I don't steal gold," he said gruffly. "People call me Honest John. I give a fair price to all." He touched the handle of the pistol. "This is so people don't steal from me." He smiled, and Amy shivered.

"I don't have anything," said Amy. "I was selling tarts, but they're all gone now."

He reached into his pocket, and pulled out a handful of gold coins. "Look at these," he said. "Double eagles. Twenty-dollar gold pieces.

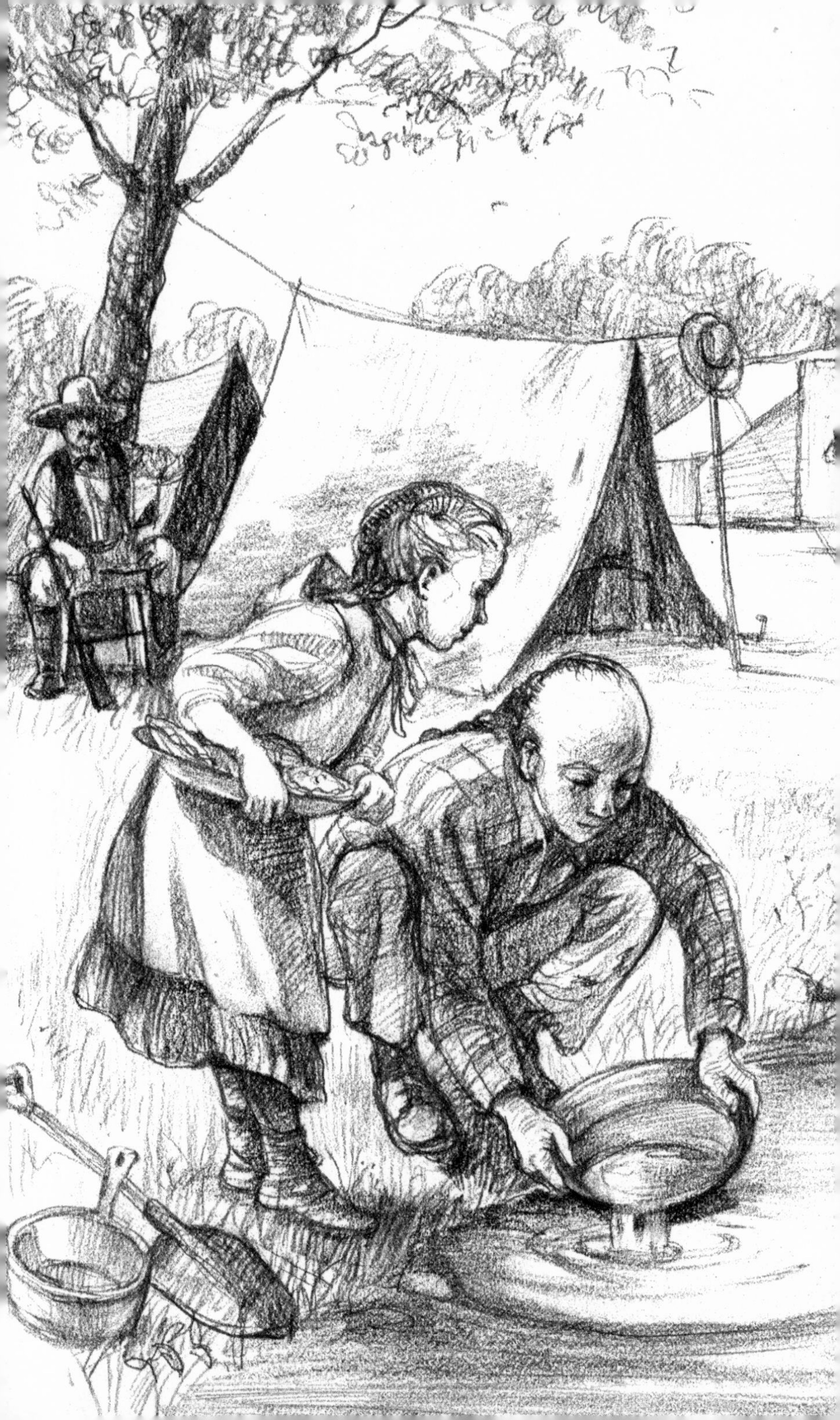

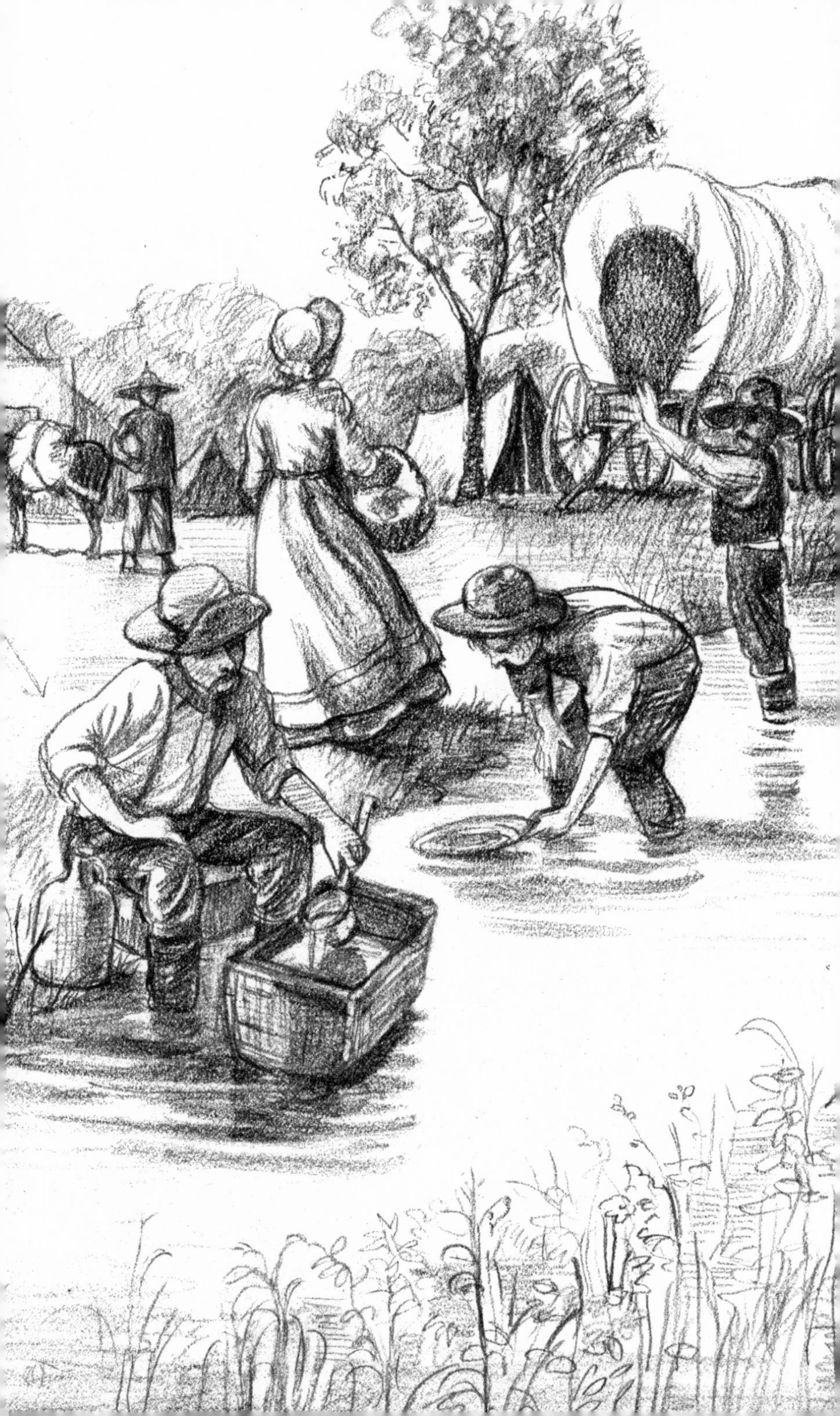

Maybe I'd give you one of these for your gold. You can buy anything you want with this."

"I don't have anything to sell," Amy said.

To Amy's relief, her mother arrived. Honest John tipped his hat and smiled. "Afternoon, ma'am," he said. "Are you selling food?"

"Well, we were," Mother said. "But I have nothing left."

"That's a shame," said Honest John. "I hear your baked goods are mighty fine. Will you be back soon?"

"Oh yes," Mother said. "We live just down the road about two miles. I'm Mrs. Harris."

"Pleased to meet you," he said. "Folks call me Honest John." He turned on his heel and went off.

Sharon soon appeared. She had sold everything too, and Mother was pleased. "We've made nearly a hundred dollars," she said.

Amy thought of the twenty-dollar gold pieces Honest John had taken from his pocket. Ten or twelve of them, and that was just pocket change for him. "Let's hurry home," she said.

On the road, Amy kept looking behind them. She was worried that Honest John would follow them. But the road was filled with people on foot, on horseback, and in wagons. Word had spread of a new gold strike, and they were rushing to be the first ones there.

"I did something terrible," Amy wrote in her diary. "And if it brings the miners to our farm, it will be all my fault. There's only one thing I can do. Find as much gold as I can before they get here. Because now I know that my rock really is gold."

CHAPTER FOUR

Gold Fever

''FATHER told us about gold fever,'' Amy wrote. "It's a kind of disease. And I think I've got it."

Amy had hoped Father would cheer up when he saw how much they had made selling baked goods. But he seemed unhappy when Mother showed him the money.

"It doesn't seem right to charge so much," he said.

"Nobody thinks it's a lot to pay," said Sharon. "When people are making fortunes in gold, they don't care how much they spend on food."

Amy bit her lip. She had wanted to tell Father that she had given the Chinese miner an apple tart, but that would only make Sharon angry.

"Very few miners are making fortunes," Father said. "And they have given up their jobs, their families . . . everything in life, to seek gold. This gold fever has affected their minds. If no one wants to grow food, or build houses, what good is gold?"

Sharon shook her head. "What good is farming? We won't be able to sell the wheat. We can't take it to be made into flour because all the mills are closed. We can only grind a little bit for ourselves. We'll starve!" She burst into tears. Father and Mother tried to comfort her, but Amy knew Sharon was just being dramatic.

Anyway, Sharon was right. They needed money. Why would it be wrong to look for gold?

So the next morning Amy took a pie pan from the kitchen. She was careful not to let anyone see her head down to the stream. Father would forgive her, she hoped, if she found enough gold.

She remembered where she had found the nugget. The stream curved just at that place, forming a pool where the water was clear. She took off her shoes and slid down the bank. A frog jumped into the water with a splash, stirring up the bottom sand.

Maybe that's a sign of luck, thought Amy. She

put the pan into the stream, right where the frog had landed. She brought it up and looked at the muddy water. She swirled it around, just the way the miner had showed her. But the water splashed out, and what remained still looked like mud. It took her a few tries to get the hang of it.

Finally she washed the mud away, leaving the heavy black sand at the bottom. She tilted the pan to catch the sun. All of a sudden she couldn't breathe.

The pan sparkled with tiny gold specks—dozens of them! Amy set it down on the edge of the bank. She tried to pick one up with her fingertip, like the miner had, but her hands were shaking too much.

Suddenly she realized that she didn't have anything to put the gold in. She ran as fast as she could back to the house. Little Fran was in the kitchen and watched in surprise as Amy grabbed an empty preserve jar.

Running back to the stream, Amy saw that Fran was following her. "Get away!" Amy shouted. Then she realized that Fran would tell Mother. Amy ran back and grabbed Fran's hand. "You can come, but don't tell anybody! It's a secret, understand?"

Back at the stream, Amy could hardly think. This is gold fever, she thought. Now she knew what it felt like. She could hardly think of anything but finding gold.

All morning Amy frantically panned in the stream. Fran learned how to pick up the flecks of gold with her fingers and put them in the jar. Amy made it seem like a game. "But don't tell!" she said. "It's going to be a surprise."

By lunchtime the jar was heavy with gold. Amy hid it under a loose board on the steps at the kitchen door. As the family ate lunch, she was excited, nervous, and afraid all at once. Fran was humming softly to herself, the way she always did when she had something to tell. Fortunately no one else noticed.

Amy had never finished her afternoon chores as quickly as she did that day. She was soon back at the stream. Fran got bored with the "game" and wandered off. But Amy didn't have time to worry about her. She was too busy filling her jar of gold.

That night she couldn't sleep. She kept trying to figure out how she could pan for gold at night. It would be too dangerous to use a lantern. Sharon might wake up and wonder where Amy had gone. This was gold fever, all right. She put her hand to her forehead, wondering if she really did have a fever. She couldn't get sick now!

For the next two days she worked as hard as she could. She filled jar after jar with the gold flakes. Then, when she awoke on the third morning, she heard Father shouting.

Amy jumped out of bed and looked out the window. Dozens of men were digging up the land around their house! Father was arguing with them. Amy couldn't hear what he was saying, but she could hear he was angry.

She slumped down on the floor. She knew why they were there. Someone—Honest John! —must have found out where the girl with the gold nugget had come from.

Sharon threw off the covers. "What's all that noise?" she said. She came to the window. "Who are these people? What are they doing?"

"They're looking for gold," said Amy.

"How stupid," said Sharon. She paused. "Maybe we ought to cook something. We can sell food right out the back door now."

Amy got dressed and went outside. Miners were everywhere. They had set up the stakes that marked their claims, even in the cornfield. Half-grown stalks of wheat were ripped up and thrown to the side. Father was arguing with a group of the miners. "This is my land," he shouted. "You have no right to be here."

They just laughed at him. "Where's your deed?" one of them said.

"Sutter rented me the land," Father replied. "I paid him for it."

"Sutter's gone broke," they said. "The land belongs to whoever wants to dig. The law is that each man can set off his own claim. You're entitled. Mark off a piece."

"I'll mark it all off," said Father.

"Too big," the miners said. "You can only mark off whatever you can work yourself. Groups can claim a bigger piece." One of the men looked at Amy. "Why don't you set up a claim with the little girl?" All the miners laughed.

Amy ran for the stream. But she was too late. Miners had already marked off sections of it. One of them was standing right where she had found the gold. He was using something she hadn't seen before. It looked like a baby's cradle, made of wood.

With a shovel, the man dumped mud from the creek into the top of the cradle. Then he rocked it back and forth, sifting the mud through a screen. He tilted the cradle, and water poured out of the other end. Then he looked into the bottom of the cradle. He smiled, and glanced around to see if anyone was watching. Seeing Amy, he winked.

She wanted to throw a stone at him. She stamped off. If only she'd thought about making a claim. But that didn't matter now. All around her were the sounds of the miners working. Shovels and pickaxes striking stones, shouts, rolling wagons—the miners had taken over. Her family's farm was ruined. And it was all her fault. By the time she reached the house, she was crying bitterly.

Honest John was waiting for her. He held out a twenty-dollar gold piece. "It's yours," he said. "Just show me where you found the gold."

Amy fled inside the house. Mother was bustling about the kitchen. "We'll have a good breakfast," she said, "and then decide what to do."

But at the table, no one spoke—not even Sharon. They were all watching Father. He didn't eat. He just sat there, staring down at the table.

Amy felt a tug at her sleeve. It was Fran. "Surprise now?" she said softly.

Amy took a deep breath. "Father," she said. "I

have to tell you something." This was harder to do than she thought it would be. "It was me . . . it was my fault that the miners came here."

Everyone looked at her in surprise. Amy got up from the table and went out to the kitchen steps. She brought back two of the jars of gold dust and set them on the table. Then two more. Father reached out and touched one of them. "Amy, what is this?" he said wonderingly.

"It's gold," she said. "I think so anyway." She took the nugget from her pocket and showed it to him. She explained about showing it to the miner at the camp. "And then they knew that gold was here, at our farm."

Father seemed stunned. "You found . . . all this?"

"Just in the last two days. In the stream. But a miner marked the place for his claim. I can't get any more."

"We don't need more!" Sharon shouted. "Don't you see? We're rich!"

Amy was angry. "Father warned us that the gold would ruin everything," Amy said. "And it has." She turned to her father. "I knew it was wrong, but I looked anyway. I had gold fever, like you said."

Father shook his head. "I must think." He

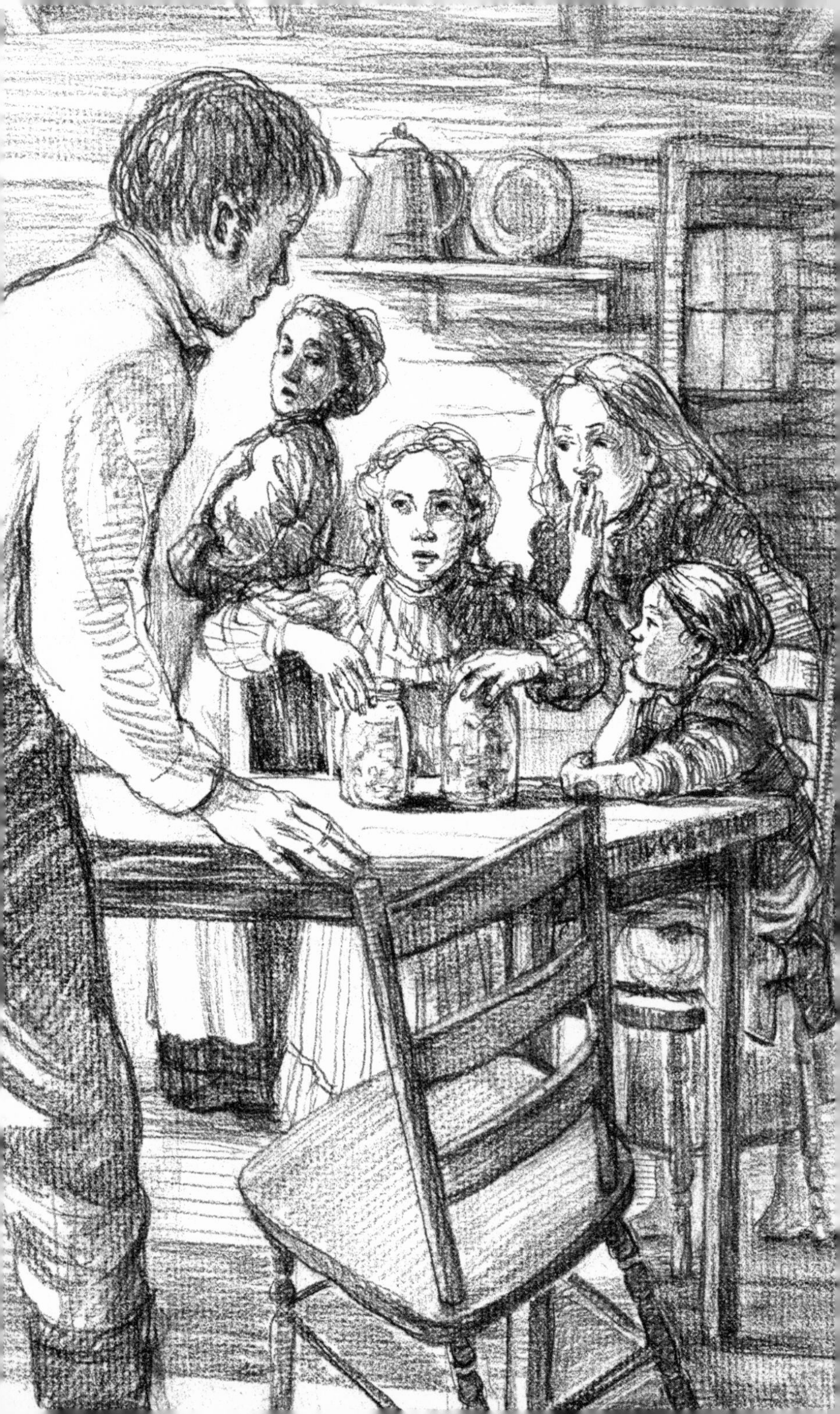

stared at the jars for a long time. Finally he spoke. "If it was here, then God must have wanted us to have it. You worked hard for it, Amy. It's yours."

"No," she said. "I want us all to have it. We can use it to start again somewhere else."

That night Amy wrote in her diary in the back of the wagon. "I'm so glad," she wrote. "Father forgave me. When he decided that it was all right to use the gold, we packed all our clothes into the wagon. And now we're headed for San Francisco. I don't know what will happen to us there, but at least we'll have money."

CHAPTER FIVE

A Ship, a Store, and a State

"EVERYTHING has changed so quickly," Amy wrote on her first night in San Francisco. "We're staying in a brand-new hotel called the Parker House. It's the grandest place I've ever seen. But Father is still worried. I'll never forget the look on his face when the desk clerk told him the price of a room was twenty dollars."

"We don't have that kind of money," Father said.

"Dear," said Mother, "we have the money from the sale of our pies."

"But that's all we have in the world," said Father.

Sharon nudged him. "Don't forget the you-know-what." She and Amy were carrying the jars of gold in a wooden box. Father nodded slowly. Amy saw that he was still not used to the idea of having lots of money.

To reach their room they walked up a carpeted staircase. Amy had never been on the second floor of a building before. She and her sisters shared a feather bed with a comforter that was filled with goose down. The walls of the room were not painted. They were entirely covered with red-and-gold-colored paper!

The next morning Amy looked out their window. It was wonderful how much you could see from up here. Hundreds of tents of all colors stood on the high hill beyond the hotel. Along the edge of the harbor there were wooden houses and stores, and dozens of men hard at work building more. And in the harbor itself were the black, bare masts of more ships than she could count. She knew that only a few hundred people had lived in San Francisco when gold was discovered. By now it had thousands, and everybody seemed busy.

When the Harrises went downstairs for breakfast, they saw several men in fancy suits coming out of a room. They left the door open, and Amy peeped inside. Several other men were seated around a table, smoking and playing cards. She stared. The table was covered with hundreds of gold coins.

Father, looking over her shoulder, pulled her away. "Gamblers!" he whispered to Mother. "This isn't a fit place for children to stay."

In the hotel dining room, they discussed what to do next. "We must find out how much the gold is worth," said Father. "I will take a small amount of it to an assayer."

"Take one of the jars," said Sharon. "We'll need a lot of money to stay here."

"We're not staying," said Father firmly. But he took the jar.

Mother and the girls went for a walk around the city. So much was happening that Amy didn't know where to look. All along the waterfront people were unloading barrels and boxes from ships. Just as quickly, wagons drew up, and shopkeepers bought the goods and hurried off.

And everywhere Amy saw the miners. Some, with new clothes and mules loaded down with tools, were leaving for the gold fields. Others, coming back, were filthy and bearded. But many of them seemed happy, and told anyone who would listen of the "big strikes" they had made. They seemed in a hurry to spend their money, and there were many storekeepers eager to take it. People had opened stores in tents and in buildings that were still being built.

Father had not returned by noon, and Mother took the girls back to the dining room for lunch. Mother's eyebrows raised when she saw the bill. She checked her bag carefully. "I hope your Father has taken care of the gold," she said.

Finally he appeared with a big smile on his face. It was so unlike him that Amy felt sure the gold must have brought a high price. She noticed that he didn't have the jar with him now.

"I have ... done something," he said. They waited to hear what it was. He swallowed, looking nervously at Mother. "I bought a ship," he said.

Sharon shot Amy a sharp glance. Amy knew what she was thinking. Father didn't know the first thing about ships. He must have gone crazy.

Then he explained. Many of the ships in the harbor had been abandoned. Their crews had run off to look for gold. Captains sold the ships to anyone for very little money.

"But now," Father said, "people have begun to pull the ships up on shore. It costs a fortune to put up a building, but you can have one ready-made with a ship."

Mother spoke gently. "But what will we do with it, dear?"

"Why, I thought we'd open a store," he said.

No one spoke. They had no idea he had such a thing in mind.

He knew what they were thinking. "I didn't make a very good farmer," he said. "And I saw how much you all enjoyed selling food to the miners. Well, then a man told me that storekeepers could do well here. You can see that."

Amy jumped up and hugged him. "It's wonderful, Father. We'll love being storekeepers."

He took them to see the ship. "There's plenty of room," he said, showing them the cabins below deck. "You can each have your own room now."

Sharon went right out and bought curtains and a rug for her room. And she bought a couple of dresses as well. Amy didn't care about those things. She chose a cabin where she could see the harbor every morning. The sea breeze came right in her window. She was glad that everybody else in the family finally seemed happy.

Mother was the one with a head for business, as Father liked to say. She went through the harbor, picking out goods that she thought the miners could use. The next day they opened the store. Before long, a young man came inside. He picked out five flannel shirts and a pair of boots. "How much?" the young man asked.

"Thirty-five dollars," Father said.

Mother frowned, but didn't say anything until the man left. "The store down the street is asking ten dollars apiece for the same shirts," she said softly. "And thirty dollars for boots."

"He didn't look like he could afford that much," Father said cheerfully. "Besides, we still made money on the sale."

The word soon spread that the Harrises' store was the best place to buy. Before long, it was filled with customers, and Mother had to buy more goods. But when she was gone, Father sometimes lent money to miners who had gone broke. "They'll pay it back when they can," he said.

One day a small man in a black suit entered the store. Mother was gone, so Amy stood next to Father as the man introduced himself. "I'm Levi Strauss," he said, extending his hand. "I've just brought a cargo of excellent cloth from France." He laid a bolt of dark blue cloth on the counter.

Amy rubbed it between her fingers. "Strong," said Mr. Strauss, smiling at her. "Heavy cotton

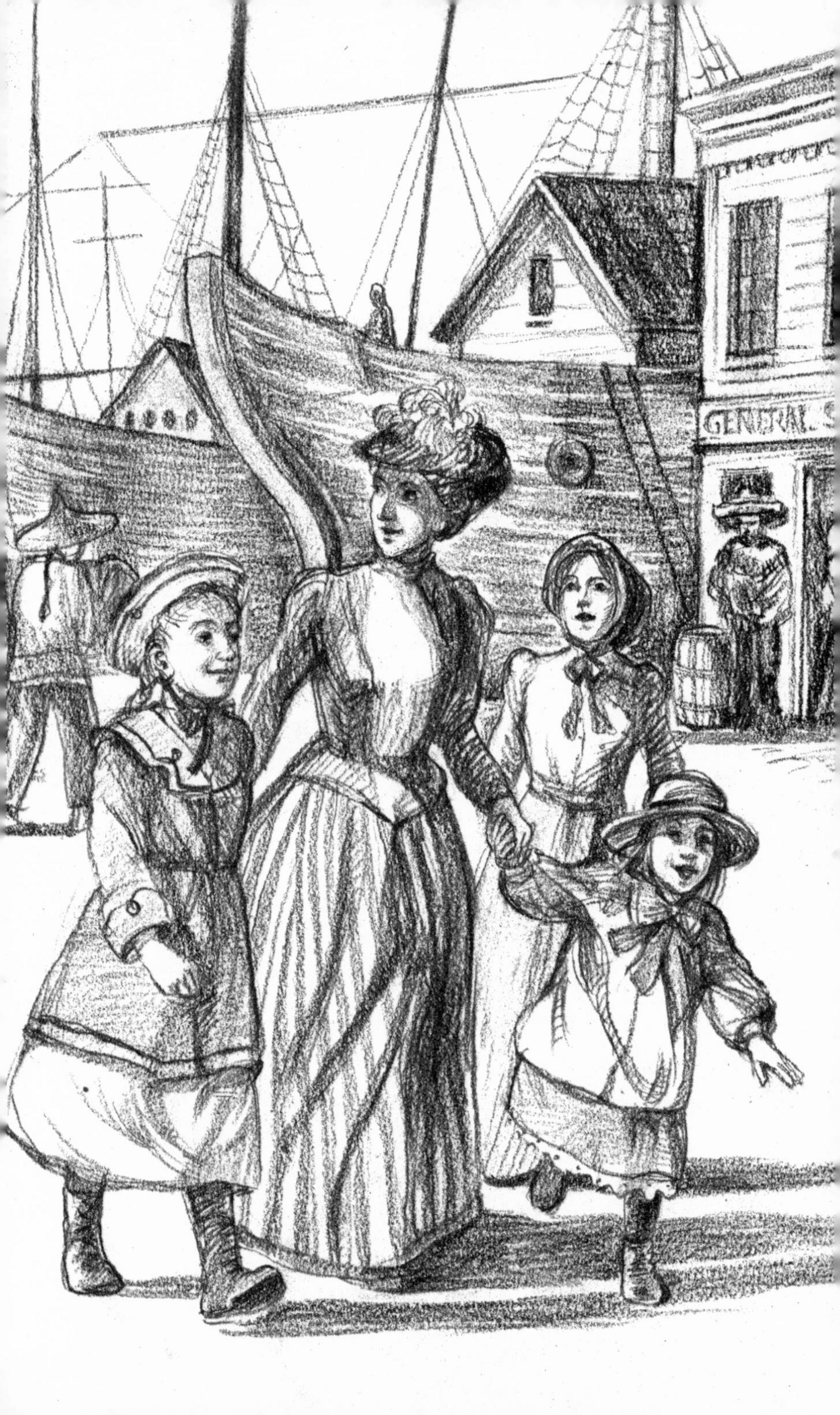
GENERAL S

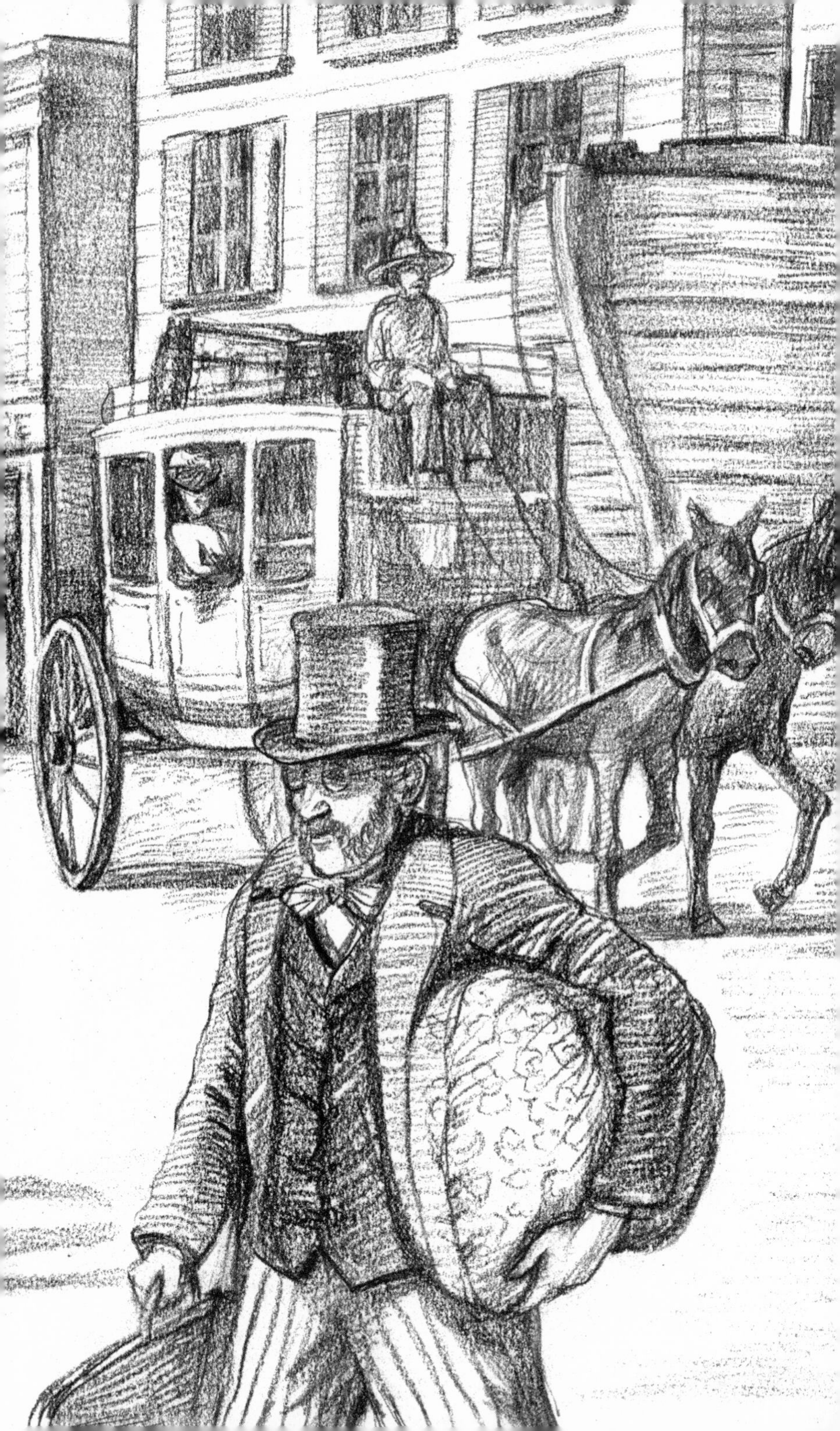

cloth made in the city of Nimes. It's called *serge de Nimes*."

Father nodded. "It's very good cloth."

"The miners could use it for their tents," said Levi Strauss. "It will keep the rain out."

One of the miners in the shop came over. He felt the cloth too. "Be good for pants," he said. "When you're standing in water all day, regular pants rot. This stuff would stand up."

"You think so?" asked Mr. Strauss. "I'll have a tailor make some pants from it."

Father said, "We'll take a dozen pairs and see how they sell."

"Maybe we should wait till Mother comes back," suggested Amy.

"Oh, she won't mind," said Father. "We can easily afford a few more pairs of pants."

"I won't forget your kindness," said Mr. Strauss.

Pretty soon the Harrises had to order more. All the miners wanted a pair of Levi's pants, which they called "denims." The Harrises made more money than ever.

Another year went by. San Francisco grew and grew, and people started to build houses on Telegraph Hill. The Harrises moved into one of them. Their business had grown so much that they needed all the room on the ship just for storage.

The house had four floors, and Amy's room was right under the roof at the top. She had a little writing desk facing the window, and on a high shelf she kept the first gold nugget that she had found. Whenever she looked at it, she thought about how lucky they had been.

They weren't the only ones. Levi Strauss had built a big factory to make more of his famous pants. He was one of the richest men in California. "You see?" Father said. "Hard work pays off." It was true. Most of those who made fortunes from the gold rush were shopkeepers.

But California was the biggest winner of all. The gold rush brought so many people there that it was soon large enough to become a state.

On October 18, 1850, Amy had a lot to write in her diary. The boom of cannons had gotten her out of bed that morning. A ship had just brought the news that California was declared a state on September 9th. For weeks people had been preparing to celebrate, and Amy dressed quickly and hurried off to her school.

Like everyone else, the Harrises closed their shop for the celebration. All through the streets people were waving American flags. Newsboys sold special editions of San Francisco's newspapers—for five dollars each.

At the parade that started at noon, everyone was carrying banners and wearing sashes of gold cloth. Soldiers marched in ranks, firing their rifles into the air. A group of Spanish *Californios* rode by on white horses. They were followed by the city's fire engines, pulled by horses decorated with flowers and streamers. Harbor workers pushed a small ship on wheels that they had built for the occasion. The Chinese people of the city tossed firecrackers and pinwheels into the streets.

Finally came a huge float drawn by six white horses. It had been made by Amy's school. Thirty children stood around the edge, each carrying the name of one of the states. Amy and Fran sat in the center, holding a big blue banner with the word *California* in gold. They waved as they saw their parents and Sharon in the crowd.

Amy was exhausted that night. But she wrote everything down in her diary, so that she would never forget. "Great things have happened to us," she wrote, "just as I dreamed they would. I will keep the gold nugget always. And when I'm an old, old lady I can show it to my grandchildren, and tell them the story of the great California gold rush of '49."

MAKING A
STAR STRING

IN SCANDINAVIA, the Christmas-New Year's season is a long one, for the long, cold winters keep people indoors much of the time. Children are kept busy making decorations like the star strings, and families are preparing smoked and pickled foods of all kinds for the great feast, or Smorgasbord, of Christmas Eve.

The season begins with the feast of St. Lucia on December 13, when the eldest daughter of the house wears a crown of candles—the name Lucia means "light."

The first Scandinavians to establish a colony in the New World were Swedes in today's Delaware. They brought the log cabin and such customs as the Yule log to America.

Materials Needed

Straw or raffia, Scissors, Warm water, Towel, Thread or string.

Steps

1. Cut the straw into three-inch lengths.
2. Moisten the straw in the water so that it will be easier to work with.
3. Protect your work table by placing the wet straws on a towel.
4. Put four of the straws side-by-side and use thread to tie them in the middle.
5. Spread the ends of the straws to make a star shape.

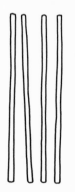  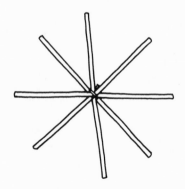

6. Repeat the process until you have enough straws to make a string of stars.

7. Tie the stars together, leaving about six inches between each one.

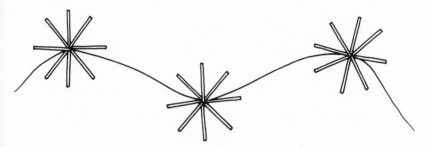

Tips

You can use wheat straw, raffia, or even paper drinking straws for the project.

If you like, you can paint the straws.

Larger and more complicated stars can be made as ornaments for a tree.